# Hoot Owl

David M. Sargent, Jr., and his friends live in Northwest Arkansas. His writing career began in 1995 with a cruel joke being played on his mother. The friends pictured with him are (from left to right) Vera, Buffy, and Mary.

Dave Sargent is a lifelong resident of the small town of Prairie Grove, Arkansas. A fourth-generation dairy farmer, Dave began writing in early December 1990. He enjoys the outdoors and has a real love for birds and animals.

# Hoot Owl

By

# Dave Sargent
## and
# David M. Sargent, Jr.

### Beyond The End
By
### Sue Rogers

Illustrated by
Jane Lenoir

Ozark Publishing, Inc.
P.O. Box 228
Prairie Grove, AR 72753

Cataloging-in-publication data

Sargent, Dave, 1941-
    Hoot Owl / by Dave Sargent ; illustrated by Jane
Lenoir. – Prairie Grove, AR : Ozark Publishing, c2003.
    vi, 42 p. : col. ill. ; 21 cm.   (Feather tale series)

    "Mind your mama" – Cover.
    SUMMARY: Young Roy the raccoon, who is going
exploring, seeks after Hoot Owl's advice but the
raccoon does not listen to what Hoot has to say.
Includes factual information about owls.
    ISBN: 1-56763-735-3  (hc)
              1-56763-736-1  (pbk)
    RL 2.4 ; IL  2-8

    [1. Owls—Fiction. 2. Raccoons—Fiction.]  I.
Lenoir, Jane, 1950-  ill. II. Title. III. Series.

    PZ10.3.S243Ho  2003
    [Fic]—dc21                                    99-059571

Printed in the United States of America

## Inspired by

my love of the freedom of wild birds and love of the very wise owls I have on my farm. They are, for the most part, barn owls.

## Dedicated to

all students who respect the owl and study hard to be wise.

## Foreword

Hoot Owl's plans for a long moonlight flight were interrupted by a ring-tailed varmint. When Hoot tries to give Roy Raccoon some good advice, Roy completely ignores him. A loud commotion and a shotgun blast follow.

# Contents

If you would like to have an author of The Feather Tale Series visit your school, free of charge, call 1-800-321-5671 or 1-800-960-3876.

# One

## Hoot Meets a Raccoon

Bright stars twinkled against the blackness of the night as the moon slowly made its appearance on the horizon. Hoot Owl was perched on a high limb of an oak tree beside the chicken house. His sleek head and body were so well groomed that he looked like a carefully molded statue. The white feathers above his eyes gave him a stern, but very wise, expression. Although it appeared that he had two little ears atop his head, they were actually tufts of feathers. He was, in fact, very impressive, sitting quietly amid the greenery of the oak tree branches. He shifted his weight from his right foot to the left as though tired of standing. He opened his big eyes, stretched his wings, and yawned. Without moving his dapple brown body, he swiveled his head from side to side, cautiously checking the barnyard for trouble spots or interesting events. But all was quiet.

"Good!" he muttered. "A nice long moonlight flight will start the night right."

As his words echoed within his mind, he chuckled.

"Hoot, you are not only a very wise old bird, but a poet as well!"

His preparation for takeoff was suddenly interrupted by a shuffling

noise and scurrying movement com-
ing up the trunk of the tree toward him.
He glared at the approaching trespass-
er and spread his wings for flight.

"Please don't leave," a youthful voice begged. "I need to talk to you."

Hoot settled back down on the tree branch and watched a furry youngster scamper across the limb toward him.

"What do you want to talk to me about?" the owl inquired in a deep voice. "And who are you?"

"I'm a raccoon, and I'm looking for some adventure," the little fellow said with a giggle. "Now, some of my friends in the woods told me that you are the wisest bird in the world."

"Hmm," Hoot thought, "I kind of like the sound of this conversation. I do believe that I am going to like this youngster!" He smiled and patted the ring-tailed lad on the head with one wing.

Hoot Owl ruffled his feathers and straightened his back as though standing at attention. The cautious little fellow scooted closer to Hoot.

"What is your name, Son?" the owl asked.

Big eyes peered from within a dark mask.

"My name is Roy Raccoon," the little critter replied. "And I want to explore the world tonight. I was told that you can tell me about any danger that is out there."

Hoot groaned and shook his head. "The world is a mighty big place, Roy Raccoon," he said quietly. "Does your mama know about your plans?"

Hoot was almost sorry he had asked when the little raccoon scooted away from him.

"I don't care how big the world is," Roy grumbled, "and my mama doesn't need to know where I am every minute!"

"You have a very bad attitude for an explorer, young fellow," Hoot exclaimed.

He flapped his wings as though preparing for takeoff.

'Oh, please don't leave," Roy whimpered.

Hoot glared at him and, in a stern voice, said, "I will stay only if you behave yourself. What do you want to know about this big world?"

"Everything!" Roy declared. Then he pointed toward the chicken house. "Say, for instance, who lives there? Why are they always sleeping? Don't they ever do anything fun?" The little fellow had a very

7

smug expression on his face as he added, "Mama said I better stay away from there, but that's silly. It doesn't look dangerous to me."

"Whoa!  Wait just a minute," Hoot said.  "You have asked a lot of questions, but you are forgetting to listen."  He glared at his headstrong student and added sternly, "And most times listening is more important than talking or exploring."

Roy watched in silence as Hoot preened his feathers and scanned the area with vigilant eyes.  After several seconds, the owl cleared his throat to speak.

"Now, young fellow, since you have decided to follow my rules, I will answer your questions.  First, that house is called a chicken house.  Chickens live there.  They sleep at night and stay awake during the day-light hours.  Farmer John and Molly depend on them for their eggs.  They are important birds on this farm!"

Roy Raccoon suddenly jumped to his feet and bolted down the trunk of the tree.

"Thanks, Hoot Owl," he barked. "Now I'm ready to see the world. First, I am going to take a good look at a real live chicken!"

"No, Roy!" Hoot Owl yelled. "Listen to your mama's advice!"

As Roy left the tree and scurried to the back of the chicken house, the wise owl shook his head and groaned, "I must warn Roy Raccoon's mama of his disobedience. The youngster does not understand the danger of his actions."

Seconds later, the magnificent bird was soaring upward into the starlit heavens.

# Two

## Varmint in the Henhouse

For almost an hour, Hoot Owl traveled in a wide circle beneath the light of the moon, frantically trying to locate Roy's mama. He looked along the banks of the river and amid the scrub oaks. He checked hollow logs and around numerous caves. Finally realizing the effort futile, he abandoned the search. "I will protect Roy Raccoon myself," he thought, "until his mama can be found."

Flying low, Hoot slowly glided toward the farmstead. Suddenly he spotted a furry figure running up the lane toward Farmer John's house.

"Whoo! Whoo!" Hoot called. "Who are you?"

The figure did not stop running, but Hoot saw her trying to find the source of the voice.

"Up here," Hoot said as he turned in a circle above her head. "I am Hoot Owl, and I am looking for the mama of Roy Raccoon."

The ring-tailed animal skidded to a stop. She looked up and saw the owl slowly circling overhead.

"I am Roy's mama," she said breathlessly. "I have been trying to find him. Do you know where he is? Is he okay? My other little ones are waiting for me beside the river, but I must not leave them alone for long. Many times I have forbidden Roy to leave the nest without telling me where he's going and when he'll be back, but he will not listen to me."

"Yes," Hoot replied, "I do know where he is, and so far, he is all right. But we need to get him away from the chicken house before he gets in real bad trouble."

"Oh my," Mama Raccoon cried. "I have warned him about staying away from there, but he will not pay attention to anything I say."

Hoot Owl was preparing to land and speak with Mama Raccoon when a loud commotion suddenly erupted near the chicken house.

The massive owl veered to the left and gained momentum. Hoot's powerful wings thrust him upward and forward at a rapid pace. His heart pounded in fear for the child raccoon as the sound of squawking chickens was joined by the irate voice of Farmer John.

"There's a dad-blamed varmint in the henhouse, Molly!" he yelled. "Run! Get my rock-salt shotgun, and I'll go see what's in there."

Hoot saw Molly running toward the house and Farmer John hurrying toward the chicken pen. Rapidly descending to ground level, he saw little Roy Raccoon. He was frozen in fear amid flying feathers, dust, and a mob of irate hens.

"Roy Raccoon!" Hoot shouted. "Move away from those chickens. I'll pick you up!"

For a split second, Hoot thought the little raccoon could not hear him. He glanced toward Farmer John who was now halfway to the chicken house.

"Roy!" he screamed. "Move away from the chickens! Now!"

As Hoot again took flight, he saw Molly running from the house with the rock-salt shotgun.

Meanwhile, little Roy Raccoon desperately fought his way to a vacant area. Rolling and tumbling toward the middle of the enclosure, the dirty and exhausted little fellow could not stand up.

Hoot circled the chicken house once before diving to the center of the pen. He grabbed Roy by the nape of his neck and lifted him high into the air. A moment later, Hoot and the wayward little critter were soaring southward.

Before reaching the safety of the forest, Hoot heard the blast from a shotgun echo amid the stillness of the night. He felt Roy quivering in fear as he gently carried him deep into the woods.

# Three

## A Lesson Well Learned

Hoot Owl searched for a safe place to land with little Roy. "If there is anything this young fellow doesn't need tonight," he thought grimly, "it's more problems." After circling an area near the river bank, Hoot Owl decided to set his precious cargo down. He gently placed him near the water's edge before settling to the ground beside him. Little Roy was breathing heavily, and his chin had been scratched by one of the alarmed chickens. Hoot Owl rubbed his beak against Roy's cheek and talked softly to him.

"You are okay now, little fellow. Just rest."

The little raccoon coughed and sat up. A tear was streaming down his cheek as he said, "I don't ever want to go exploring again! And I don't like Farmer John and Molly any more. They are mean!"

The little ring-tailed raccoon went into a spasm of wails and sobs. "I don't like them, and I hope they shot themselves in their feet!"

"Whoa! Wait a minute," Hoot said. "The problems that you had tonight were of your own making. Farmer John and Molly are good people. You are the one who insisted on exploring. You refused to listen to your mama or me! You didn't want to know the truth about the dangers that are out in the big world. You just wanted to do your own thing!" Hoot paused just long enough to catch his breath before adding, "And you did that all right. Now, will you admit that your mama is wiser to the ways of the world than you?"

The nod of little Roy's head was accompanied by a sob and a hiccup.

"I'm sorry, Hoot," he sniffled. "I guess I still have a lot to learn before I can be a good explorer. I just want my mama. Do you know where she is?"

Suddenly the owl remembered that Mama Raccoon was nearly to the farm when the commotion in the chicken pen occurred. His heart was filled with fear for her safety. He looked down at little Roy without responding to the question.

"What's wrong, Hoot?" the little raccoon asked. "My mama's okay, isn't she?'

"I think so, Roy," Hoot Owl said quietly. "I have something to say, and I want you to listen carefully. It is very important that you listen to every word.'

"Yes, I'll listen," Roy agreed.

"I want you to stay right here while I go check on your mama. Do you hear me, Roy Raccoon?" Hoot added sternly, "Do not move from this spot!"

"I won't move," Roy Raccoon
said. "I promise."

Thirty minutes later, Hoot and Mama Raccoon were standing beside Roy. The little fellow had not moved one inch from the spot that he had been assigned. He squealed with delight and hugged his mama.

"I promise to listen to you, Mama," he vowed. "You and my friend Hoot are much wiser than me."

Hoot Owl smiled and winked at Mama Raccoon.

"I do believe that Roy has learned the importance of your rules tonight," Hoot said warmly. "You behave yourself, my little friend Roy, and perhaps we will meet again one day."

A moment later, Hoot was airborne. "It is sad," he thought, "that the little fellow had to learn his lesson the hard way."

"I can't help but wonder what the little fellow will get into next time!" he muttered with a smile. Hmmm . . .

# Four

## Owl Facts

We use the name *owl* for birds that are members of a certain group of nocturnal birds of prey. There are two families in this group: owls, like Hoot, which we are used to seeing, have about 167 species; and barn owls, which have around 14 species. There are differences in the anatomy of the two families of owls, but many generalizations apply to both.

The eyes of barn owls are just a little smaller than other owls. They are directed forward, and are sort of encased in a capsule of bone called the sclerotic ring. They barely move their eyes. They turn their entire head when they look sideways. The neck is long and flexible. This permits the head to rotate 270 degrees. Most owls' eyes are surrounded by a facial disk of stiff feathers.

BARN OWL

270°

Because only a few owls hunt their prey in daylight, their hearing is extremely important. Many owls have asymmetrical skulls, with ear openings at different levels; this lets the bird get a "fix" on the sound made by the little animal they are after.

Owls are found all over the globe except in the Antarctic region. The common barn owl, like those we have around the United States, has one of the largest ranges of all living birds. The nesting habits of owls are very different. Some nest in holes in trees or among rocks. Others nest in large tree-nests. Owls like burrowing owls nest on the ground. All owls lay pure white eggs.

All owls feed on living animals, and the size of the prey will match the size of the owl. They eat everything from insects to mammals as big as hares. A few feed mainly on fish. Parts of food, such as bones, feathers, and hair, are mostly indigestible. They are compressed and then are regurgitated as compact pellets. The pellets prove their prey's species.

Some genera of owls have many species, with the largest genus containing more than 50. Some owls of this genus are very well known, like the eastern screech owl of the eastern part of North America, and the Eurasian scops owl. This species migrates. These owls breed in southern Europe and east to Lake Baikal. Many of the tropical species of owls are known from only a few museum specimens, and their habits have not yet been studied. All species that belong to the largest genus of owls look much alike, and, as expected in nocturnal birds, are differentiated by their very distinctive voices.

Eagle owls are one of the largest species of owls. They have tufts of feathers on their heads. These tufts are called "ears" but are not true ears.

The great horned owl is found mostly in North and South America, but there are 17 species in Europe, Africa, and Asia. The northern eagle owl is found from Scandinavia and Spain to Japan. The northern eagle owl is about 28 inches long.

The elf owl of the southwestern United States and Mexico is 5 inches

GREAT HORNED OWL

NORTHERN EAGLE OWL

long and is the smallest member of
the family.   It nests in woodpecker
holes in large cacti.
    Scientific Classification: Our
typical owls, like Hoot, make up the

family *Strigidae,* and barn owls make up the family *Tytonidae.* Common barn owls are classified as *Tyto alba,* and burrowing owls are classified as *Speotyto cunicularia.* The largest genus of owls is *Otus.* (We don't know if you will ever need this information, but it may come in handy.) The eastern screech owl is classified as *Otus asio.* Eurasian scops owls are classified as *Otus scops.* Eagle owls make up the genus *Bubo.* The great horned owl is classified as *Bubo virginianus,* and the northern eagle owl as *Bubo bubo.* Elf owls are classified as *Micrathene whitneyi.* And you thought Hoot was just a common ole owl, didn't you?

# BEYOND "THE END" . . .

## LANGUAGE LINKS

dapple brown body
shuffling noise
scurrying movement
furry youngster
wisest bird
headstrong student
vigilant eyes
important birds
magnificent bird
scrub oaks
massive owl
squawking chickens
irate hens
precious cargo
alarmed chickens

What five words in the list above
describe Hoot Owl?

What five words describe Roy Raccoon and some things he did?
What four words describe the chickens?
What does the other word describe?

These important and wonderful words are called adjectives. Without them we would not have known how Hoot and Roy looked, or how upset the chickens got. These adjectives described a noisy commotion a "dad-blamed varmint" caused in the hen-house.

# CURRICULUM CONNECTIONS

Popular myth suggests that owls are blind in the daylight when in fact they are not. What is a myth?

Compare a human eye with the eye of an owl. See <www.stlukeseye. com/Anatomy.asp> for the anatomy of a human eye. Then look at <www.owlpages.com/physiology/ vision.html> for a diagram of an owl eye. How are they alike? How are they different?

Use only the number cards in a deck of cards. Get a partner, or partners, and play NUMBER WAR. Give each player an equal number of cards. Each player turns over two cards. The player with the highest

SUM wins all the cards turned over. When a player runs out of cards to turn over, he or she picks up the cards he or she has won and uses them. Play continues until one player has all the cards and wins the WAR!

A study revealed that a barn owl eats, over the course of a year, 1407 mice, 143 rats, 7 bats, 5 young rabbits, 375 house sparrows, 23 starlings, 54 other birds, 4 lizards, 174 frogs, 25 moths, and 52 crickets. Check my figures, but when I add all these numbers together, I get 2,269 pieces of food! What an appetite! How many days are there in a year? How many pieces did the barn owl eat each day of the year? Does this make a barn owl a help or a pest on a farm? Why?

# THE ARTS

You learned on one of the web sites above how the owl moves his head, rotating it 270 degrees and almost turning it upside down. He has a long and very flexible neck. He cannot turn his eyes.

Pretend that you are a wise ole owl, sitting on a branch high up in a tree. Turn on some music. Moving nothing but your head, Wise Owl, dance with the music!

# THE BEST I CAN BE

Read the dedication page again. It sounds like this book is dedicated to you. You do study to be wise and you do keep your body well groomed, don't you? So the book is dedicated to you—to applaud the high standards you have set for your life! Pat yourself on the back!